what
the
Sea
Saw

For my parents, who taught me to love the sea,
and my children, with whom I have shared that love.
—S. St. P.

To my husband, Dean,
whose loving patience allows me freedom to work,
and to my unpredictable horse, Nate,
who keeps me sane while I'm working.
—B. D.

Published by
PEACHTREE PUBLISHERS
1700 Chattahoochee Avenue
Atlanta, Georgia 30318-2112

www.peachtree-online.com

Text © 2006 by Stephanie St. Pierre
Illustrations © 2006 by Beverly Doyle

Art direction by Loraine M. Joyner
Typesetting by Melanie McMahon Ives

Illustrations created in airbrush on illustration board.

Printed in Singapore
10 9 8 7 6 5 4 3 2 1
First Edition

Library of Congress Cataloging-in-Publication Data

St. Pierre, Stephanie.
  What the sea saw / written by Stephanie St. Pierre ; illustrated by Beverly Doyle.-- 1st ed.
    p. cm.
  Summary: A lyrical introduction to the sea, its inhabitants, and its role in the world around it. Includes facts about the ecosystems of oceans and shorelines.
  ISBN 1-56145-359-5
  [1. Ocean--Fiction. 2. Coasts--Fiction. 3. Sea birds--Fiction. 4. Marine animals--Fiction. 5. Marine ecology. 6. Ecology.] I. Doyle, Beverly, 1963- ill. II. Title.
  PZ7.S14355Wha 2006
  [E]--dc22
                                        2005027192

What
the
Sea
Saw

Written by
Stephanie St. Pierre

Illustrated by
Beverly Doyle

PEACHTREE
ATLANTA

What the sea saw was sky above.

What the sky saw was sea below.

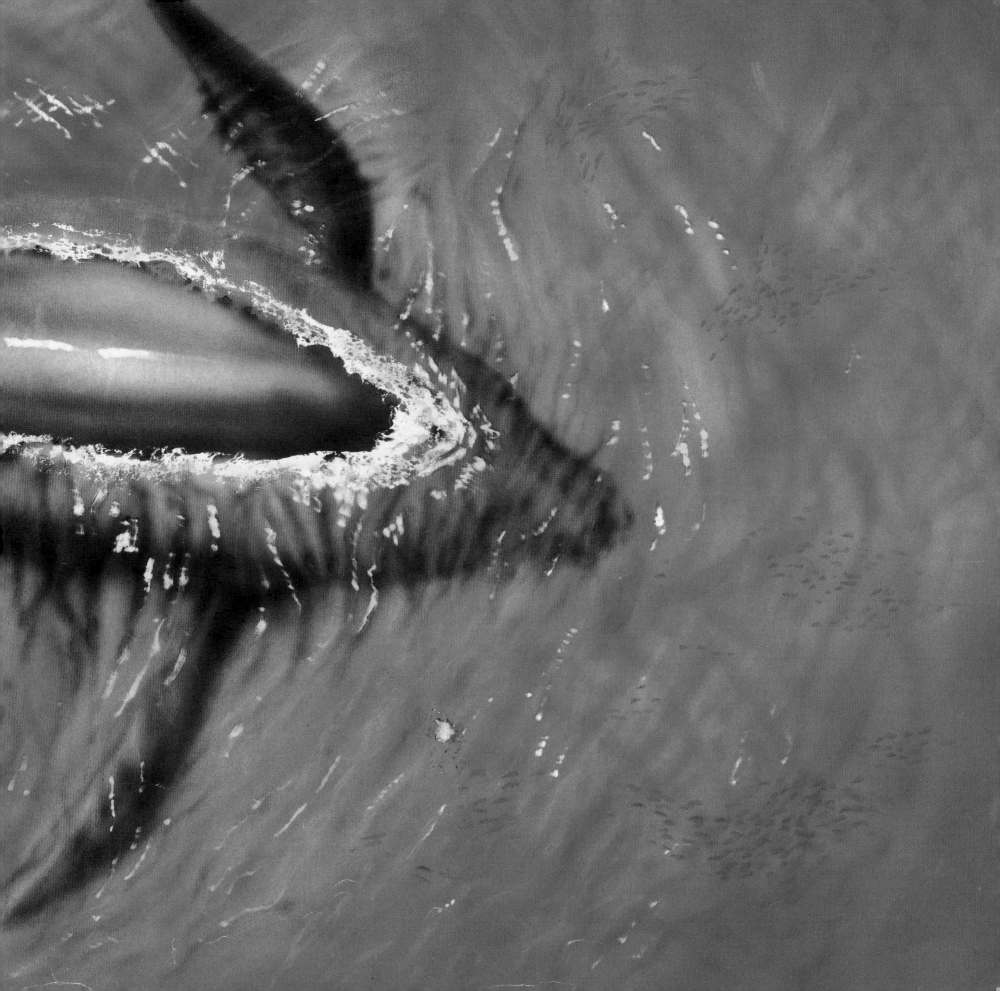

The sea saw

a gull shoot from the sky

leaving the wind empty.

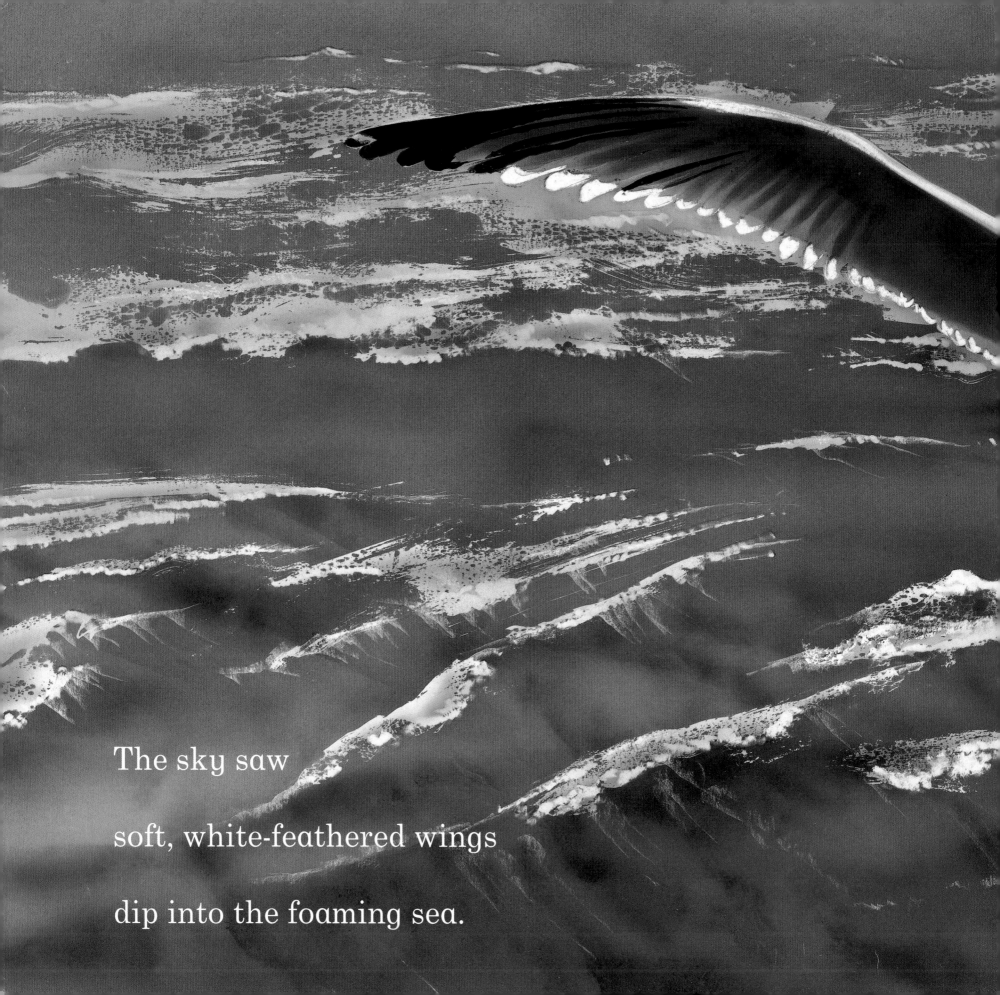

The sky saw

soft, white-feathered wings

dip into the foaming sea.

The gull saw

fish in the sea swimming in schools,

scales shimmering silver.

The fish saw

light on the waves

weaving into the deep.

And down in the deep,

perfect pink shells,

stringy seaweed gardens,

lobsters with clamping claws,

crabs scuttling,

oysters scooting...

...a lone shark on the move.

The sea crashed against giant rocks,

splashing and foaming,

leaving treasures behind

in tiny pools that mirrored the sky.

Sandpipers ran

across the wet sand

leaving a trail

of three-pronged footprints.

The gull screeched

and flew through the heavy sky.

Clouds gathered and burst,

sending the sky falling over the rocks,

into the sea and onto the hot, dry sand.

Along the dunes the rain fell

on beach plums ripened in the sun,

on purple thistle prickles,

and soft pink petals...

...tangled in a spider's silk.

The sea saw

sand on the shore,

round rocks rubbed smooth,

and starfish clinging.

The sky saw

the moon rising round

through the purple night full of stars.

The sea saw

a ring around the moon.

The sky saw

a dolphin leaping.

Sky above.

Sea below.

An ecosystem is a combination of plants and animals that exist together in a particular place in nature. Many different habitats can be a part of the same ecosystem. The ecosystem at the seashore includes habitats in the water, at the shore, and in the dunes. These areas are home to groups of plants and animals that have adapted to different conditions of water, light, and temperature. These conditions affect the way plants and animals breathe and eat and grow. By exploring the seashore you can learn more about the plants and animals that live there.

In the Water Most ocean plants and animals are found in three different areas: the shallow bottom near the shore, the sunny water near the surface, and the deeper waters of the open ocean.

In the sunny surface waters, millions and millions of tiny plants and animals float. They are too small to see without a microscope. These creatures are called plankton. They are food for many other creatures that live in the sea.

Creatures that live in the shallow bottom near the shore must be able to survive the pounding surf. Hard shells protect the soft bodies of creatures like crabs and clams.

In the deep waters of the open sea, creatures can grow to be very large. They must be good swimmers, like the dolphin.

eco-tip: Be careful not to leave trash behind at the beach. Garbage is one of the many kinds of pollution that can harm plants and animals that live in and around the sea.

At the Shoreline At the shoreline animals and plants adapt to fill every niche in the environment: in the sand, in areas where the tide is sometimes very high and sometimes very low, and in small pools of water on rocks and cliffs. Each of these areas is very different, and creatures that can exist in one niche may die if moved to another. Some creatures dig down deep into the shore where the sand stays cool and wet all the time.

Some creatures in a rock pool survive on top of a rock. Others can only live beneath the same rock.

While exploring it is important to leave things as you find them. Turning over a small rock and forgetting to put it back the way you found it could destroy the habitat for all the animals and plants that live on or under it.

eco-tip: When collecting shells be sure to take only those that are empty. Look and leave living creatures where you find them.

On the Dunes Wind blowing inland from the sea causes the erosion of soil and leaves a salty sandy area by the sea where most plants cannot grow. There are a few hardy grasses that can grow in these areas. These grasses help turn the dunes into a better habitat for other plants and animals.

Over time, plants like beach plums and thistle will take root. Then small animals like rabbits, mice, and songbirds come to eat the leaves and seeds of these plants. Larger animals like foxes hunt the smaller ones and scavenge at the shore for dead fish and crabs.

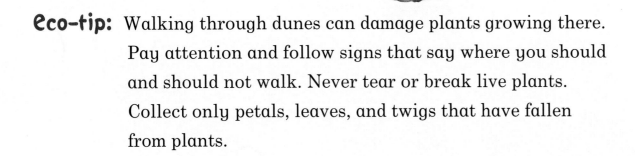

eco-tip: Walking through dunes can damage plants growing there. Pay attention and follow signs that say where you should and should not walk. Never tear or break live plants. Collect only petals, leaves, and twigs that have fallen from plants.

The illustrator found the following books to be especially helpful in developing the paintings for WHAT THE SEA SAW.

A BEACH FOR THE BIRDS by Bruce McMillan (Houghton Mifflin/Walter Lorraine Books)

BENEATH THE NORTH ATLANTIC by Jonathan Bird (Tide-Mark Press)

BUTTERFLIES OF NORTH AMERICA by Jim Brock and Ken Kaufman (Houghton Mifflin)

GULLS by Bill Ivy (Grolier Academic Reference)

OCEAN LIFE by Sally Morgan and Pauline Lalor (PRC Publishing)

SEABIRDS by John Mackenzie (Key Porter Books)

SHOREBIRDS: FROM STILTS TO SANDERLINGS by Sara Swan Miller (Franklin Watts)

KIRKWOOD

7-28-06